THE

IMMIGRANT

A Journey of Sacrifices & Survival. Where Dreams
Collide with the Reality

i

First Edition: 2024

Publication Month: October

THE

IMMIGRANT

A Journey of Sacrifices & Survival. Where Dreams
Collide with the Reality

BY

HABIB AHMED

CONTENTS

CHAPTER 1

My heart pounded relentlessly against my ribs, each beat echoing in my ears like a thunderclap. My hands were as cold as ice, numb and unresponsive as if they had been clutching a fistful of snow for hours. I put my hand under my armpits. We were huddled together so tightly that I had to squeeze between the people to move. My body was numb, paralyzed by the chilly winds that seeped into the very marrow of my bones. I was trembling uncontrollably, unable to tell whether it was hunger, fear, or cold that caused my body to vibrate incessantly. The air was thick with a pungent blend of scents. I could smell the greasy aroma of stale, soggy shawarma wafting from a nearby container, the mingled sweat of a multitude of bodies, the tang of unwashed socks, the subtle fragrance of women's perfumes, and traces of incense. Apart from that, the air was filled with a cacophony of sounds: the weary breaths of the passengers mingling with the wheezing coughs, the soft murmuring of prayers, the chatter of restless children, and the insistent cry of an infant. These voices were intensifying the palpable tension that hung heavy in the air. In a matter of a few minutes, a powerful wave surged from the ocean, causing the boat to swing and tilt precariously, half-submerged in the water. A sudden, dread-filled scream echoed across the boat, shattering the fragile silence and sending shivers down our spines. Yet, amidst this symphony of chaos, a delicate sound pierced the gloom, a beacon of hope amid despair. It had been the tinkling of my wife's bangles. This familiar melody echoed through my mind, evoking memories of our home, a place of warmth and comfort. The sound had been like a lifeline, a reminder of the love that bound us—a love that anchored me amidst the storm.

Suddenly, a glimmer of light pierced the darkness, momentarily blinding me. The sudden brightness sent a jolt of fear across the boat. I instinctively tightened my grip on my wife. In a few moments, we reached the shore. Two men, holding torches against the boat, stood in the distance, their forms outlined by the flickering flames. They stood attentively, like seasoned military officers. They had microphones tucked into their ears and walkie-talkies in their hands. One of them held the microphone close to his mouth and uttered something into it. The boatman instructed us to disembark. People scrambled to their feet, grabbed their belongings, and hastily alighted from the boat one by one.

My legs turned to lead, refusing to obey as I tried to stand. It felt like an eternity before I could wobble upright, my muscles screaming in protest. Taking a deep breath, I kneeled, gathering our belongings with trembling hands. The weight of the bag seemed to pull me back down, but I hoisted it onto my shoulder with a grunt. Then came the most precious cargo—our daughter. I gently lifted her from my wife's lap, her slight form snuggling close against my chest. Her tiny arms wrapped around my neck, a silent plea for comfort in this strange new world. With a reassuring smile, I offered my hand to my wife. Her eyes, mirroring my own determination, met mine. We shared a silent promise, a pact to face whatever awaited us together. Hand in hand, we rose, the movement slow but steady. As the last stragglers stumbled ashore, we followed, leaving the boat and its promise of escape behind. The unknown stretched before us, vast and uncertain, but the warmth of our family bond was a beacon of hope in the gathering darkness.

My eyes darted around, taking in my surroundings. We were standing in the heart of a dense, forbidding forest, its towering trees forming an impenetrable wall around us. The dreary ocean we had just crossed lay behind us. Two men, clad in black suits, emerged from the two black vans parked nearby and walked toward us. A man with a long, symmetrical face, captivating hazel eyes that sparkled like the moon over the ocean, sleek, shiny brown hair parted to one side and slicked back with gel, and a high-bridged nose strode past us. After a few steps, he turned back and fixed his piercing gaze on me, sending a jolt of heat through my body. I stood my ground because I knew I had no reason to be afraid, for I had not forgotten who I was. I met his unwavering stare, and he smirked before moving on. The other person, with curly black hair, a thick mustache, and narrowed brown eyes, approached the boatman.

"How many people?"

"Thirteen," he replied firmly.

The man nodded and handed a white postal envelope to the boatman. "Count them."

He hesitated for a moment, then reluctantly counted the money. "Fits," he muttered.

"Leave now."

Meanwhile, the man with hazel-blue eyes began herding us into two matte black VW vans. There were no seats inside, and we were crammed in tightly, pushed, and shoved until the doors slammed shut. My legs were squeezed against my body, one arm pressed against the door, and the other protectively wrapped around my wife, holding our daughter tightly against her chest. One-way windows were installed in the cars, allowing me to glimpse where we were headed. We were traveling along a very thin road deep into the heart of the jungle. Only a few lights flickered weakly, casting an eerie glow on the dark road. The ominous black clouds loomed in the sky, threatening to unleash their torrents of rain. The people in the van were gasping for air due to the lack of ventilation. When the driver lowered the window, a gust of fresh air swept through the cramped space, offering us a momentary respite. We crossed the jungle in an hour and traveled on the motorway for a while when sometimes the other black van traveling with parted way drove off the motorway. After what seemed like an eternity of traveling miles on the motorway, the van took a sharp turn and pulled up in front of a large, imposing cottage. The few security guards stationed outside straightened up as they saw the approaching vehicle. One of the guards in charge signaled to his colleagues, and they rushed to open the gate. The van came to a halt, and the man in the black suit emerged from the driver's seat. He opened the van door, and we surged out like a flock of sheep released from their pen.

CHAPTER 2

In front of me was a two-story cottage with a brown hip roof and whitewashed walls. Two hung windows were installed on each side, with a few centimeters of distance between them at the entrance door of the cottage. The two cars were parked on the porch: one was a sleek black Mercedes Maybach, and the other was a red Fiat SUV. On the left side of the porch, a hip-high picket fence extended along a door that led to an apple farm stretching for about one to two miles. Workers were plucking ripped, juicy, red apples. I assumed that most of them were Middle Eastern and Southeast Asian, primarily Pakistanis, Indians, Bengalis, and a few African natives. They then placed them in single-wheel trolleys. When the trolleys were full, they signaled to others, who then pushed the trolleys toward people laying and arranging the apples in crates. A few were assigned to fill the truck with these crates.

The man with hazel blue eyes approached one of the truck drivers, an older man with hooded eyes, a flat nose, thick lips, and deep wrinkles surrounding his mouth. He was likely in his fifties, leaning against the truck and smoking a cigarette.

"Hey, Jack," the truck driver greeted with a wide smile, playfully punching Jack's chest. "Where were you, dude?"

"I've brought a consignment for you," Jack replied, getting straight to the point.

The smile vanished from the driver's face as he directed them to load the crates onto the truck.

Jack signaled to someone nearby, and that person approached him. After a brief exchange, they came to us. "Get on the truck," Steven instructed.

Zariya held my arm tightly, and I clenched my fists, tumultuous emotions churning within me. I questioned my presence in this place, wondering how circumstances had led me to feel shackled by these circumstances. I closed my eyes and felt the veins in my temples throbbing as I thought about who was to blame for my suffering. I had not chosen this life, this journey, or this fate. The war and those in power had forced it upon me. My train of thought was interrupted by the sound of Aleha crying.

"Shhh, Aleha, keep quiet, habibiti," Zariya comforted, patting her swiftly.

"Stop this bloody, cranky voice!" Jack exclaimed.

She immediately covered her mouth. We squeezed into the truck, surrounded by crates of apples. The darkness behind the crates made me contemplate holding Zariya's hand and running away from where we belonged.

A loud, irritated voice boomed from behind the crates.

"What happened?" One of the men asked.

"A crate fell down!" an older man replied sheepishly.

"You careless old fool!" Jack roared, his voice echoing through the truck. "Are you too blind to see this massive tray? Pick it up and get moving!"

"Yes, sir," the old man mumbled, scrambling to retrieve the fallen crate.

"And hurry up!" Jack barked, his voice laced with impatience.

Someone lowered the heavy shutter, plunging the truck into an oppressive darkness. The truck then started moving forward on the straight, paved road. The interior was dark and silent, so dark that you couldn't even make out the person sitting next to you. The truck traveled uninterrupted for two to three hours until it was pulled over. I could hear someone talking in a thick British accent, but I couldn't understand much of what they were saying. The shutter of the truck was rolled up. In the beam of light piercing through the hole between the crates, I could see my wife resting her head on my shoulder. The discomfort was evident on her forehead, and her little nose was scrunched up, just as she usually did when upset about something. Her eyes were tightly shut, which made the skin around the edges of her eyes fold. Perhaps she had just had a nightmare, or perhaps she was still having one. Then I glanced at Aleha, sleeping soundly in her mother's arms, secure in the knowledge that no harm could reach her as long as it had to pass through her mother first. For a moment, I wished I could forget the scene that flashed before my eyes—the bodies of my Mama and Baba, pulled out of the rubble of our house, smeared with cement and dirt, and covered with a silvery and white film. Baba's spleen was pierced with an iron rod that passed in and out of his body; his face was spattered with blood, and his lifeless body hung in the arms of the worker who had pulled him out of the rubble. Mama's *khalat* was soaked in blood, her hand was cut off, her feet were swollen as if they would burst, and her body was crushed beyond recognition.

After a few moments, the shutter was rolled down, and again, I could hear some chatter—the convincingly assuring voice of the driver. I believe the other person was convinced because, after a few movements, we were again moving in our direction. I was tired and hungry, my head was heavy, and my body was stiff, so I dozed off—just as in childhood when I was sad and had done something I didn't want to face the consequences of. I used to fall asleep as if, when I'd wake, everything would have passed, and everything would become normal again. Today, too, I desperately wanted everything to be the same as it was before. I wished not to wake up again, but I know that I have to wake up again. My world is not yet destroyed because I have Zariya and Aleha, and we will create our world again here—not the same as the previous one, but maybe a peaceful one.

CHAPTER 3

I found myself standing in a warehouse. On the left side of the warehouse was a long, slender table draped in a plastic orange and white checkered sheet. On both sides of the table, individuals were standing, filling small plastic sachets with white powder and sliding them to the edge. A person then placed the sachets of white powder on the surface of a brown cardboard box and filled the rest of the box with apples, covering them with brown paper on top. This completed package was then passed along to other workers, who sealed it and affixed an etiquette label.

Meanwhile, others stacked the boxes onto a dolly. About twenty-five individuals were working in the warehouse. On the other side of the warehouse, partitioned with brown cotton curtains, numerous thin mattresses were laid. Each mattress had folded blankets and bags placed on it, and plastic disposable plates with leftovers were scattered beside the mattresses.

Amidst the hubbub, a man with green eyes, a shoulder-length beard, and a muscular physique approached us. He towered over me, standing at least three or four inches taller. With a firm hand, he placed it on my shoulder as I gently pushed Zariya behind me.

"Welcome to the UK," he declared in a gruff voice. He took two steps back and shouted, "Everyone, stand still! Don't move!" He turned his attention back to me and demanded, "You there! What's your name?"

I held my breath and replied, "Rayan."

"Put the bag down," he ordered in a low, menacing tone.

I knew that arguing with this man would be futile and could potentially put my family in danger. So, I removed the bag from my shoulder and placed it on the ground.

Zariya gently grabbed my shoulder and whispered, "Hold it, give it to me."

I shook my head reassuringly. "No, no... it's fine," I whispered.

The man stepped forward. "Why did you bring this? Did you come here for a picnic?" he barked.

"There is milk and some other things in it for my daughter," I explained.

The man's expression hardened. "Don't you dare bring anything into this place that isn't for work!" he snapped, his voice dripping with menace.

Just then, a man in a black office pants and coat emerged from the shadows. He was short, barely 5'4", with a potbelly, olive skin, hooded eyes, and a small nose. His slicked-back black hair had an undercut, and he was chewing betel quid. A worker followed him, carrying a vase and standing behind him.

The man surveyed the scene with a cold, calculating gaze. "What's the matter, Steven?" he asked in a deep, gravelly voice.

Steven replied, "Nothing, Boss. The new batch of workers has arrived. There are six of them in total." He leaned back, nodded his head, and spoke in a voice so low it seemed to echo from the depths of a valley.

The boss turned around in a circle, surveying us, and said, "I see."

Steven immediately raised his head and said hurriedly, "You all introduce yourselves to the boss one by one."

The boss shook his head. "No need for an introduction, Steven... there are none from my IN Laws; take them and start the work."

Steven nodded and said, "Yes, boss!"

The boss turned and headed back to his office. Steven then turned to us and led us toward the packaging area. He signaled to his workers and addressed us, "This will be your workplace from now on. Understand? Before you start working, I need to lay down some ground rules. First, no excuses will be tolerated. We need healthy workers. If you're sick or unwilling to work, you will be given a permanent vacation and can relax in heaven. You will work seventeen hours a day, with no days off. You will not be allowed to leave this place; there will be no mobile phones or internet access, and you will have to cut off all ties with the outside world. You will be given two meals a day. As you have already seen, we are involved in drug smuggling. The white packets you see are drugs, and they are packed with apples and sealed immediately before being transported across the country and distributed through a chain of drug dealers. If anyone has any objections, speak up now."

The room fell silent. Everyone's faces were etched with fear and shock as if they had just been handed death sentences. I, however, remained composed, for I had expected something like this. I knew no one would take such a risk transporting us here without expecting something in return. Every favor has a hidden agenda, and every penny spent getting us here would undoubtedly be recouped through exploitation. I resolved not to participate in this illegal activity, no matter the consequences.

"I object!" I declared, my voice cutting through the tense silence. "I did not come here to engage in this type of work. The agent promised us a decent job."

Steven scoffed. "Should we make you Prime Minister then? Listen, Rayan, you have no choice. If you want to stay here, you have to do what everyone else does. You're an illegal immigrant in this country, and you have nowhere else to go. If you try to escape and the police catch you, you'll be imprisoned and deported back to your homeland. So don't get any ideas. Just start working."

His words sent a shiver down my spine, but my resolve remained unshaken. I would not be coerced into participating in this immoral activity. I turned around, took Zariya's hand, and headed towards the gate, retrieving my bag from the ground as we left.

A murmur rippled through the workers as Steven shouted from behind, "STOP!"

I turned to face him as he approached, reached into his pocket, pulled out a card, and placed it in my palm. "Call me when you change your mind," he said. "You're the only one I'm giving a second chance to. I admire your courage, but, my boy, you've shown it to the wrong people. In a few days, you'll be dead. I hope you reach out to me soon."

His words hung heavy in the air, a chilling reminder of the dire consequences of my defiance. Yet I remained undeterred. I would not compromise my principles, no matter the cost.

A worker approached Steven, his expression anxious. "Steven, you can't let them go! What if they go to the police?"

Steven chuckled dismissively. "Don't worry, buddy. They're illegal immigrants, and they'll be arrested as soon as the police find out. Do you really think he'd be so stupid as to go to the police?" He turned to me and Zariya, a sly grin spreading across his face. "Right, Rayan?"

CHAPTER 4

We were walking down a bustling street when it got a lot darker than when we left the warehouse, which I believe only took about thirty minutes. I glanced at the tower clock's striking hands; it read five o'clock. The biting wind sent a chill through my body despite my layers of warm clothing. We were not dressed for a European chill; I was in black jeans, a blue check shirt, and beige woolen sweaters layered under a summer jacket, while Zariya adorned herself in a vibrant red knee-length shawl wrapped around her neck and trailing down her body, a black scarf on her head, and black trousers. Zariya had bundled Alia warmly in a bay pink beanie and mittens, two sweaters, and a jacket. We had been instructed by the agents not to bring any luggage, leaving us with only Alia's milk bottle, powder, and a few snacks for her.

It had been over twenty-four hours since we had eaten or drank anything. Zariya's unsteady gait and slow pace revealed she had the power to walk; I felt a pang of guilt for subjecting her to this ordeal. I had persuaded her to come with me after our home was destroyed by an airstrike that killed my Mama and Baba. Our belongings—my father's lifelong investment, the fruits of his hard work and sweat—were reduced to rubble in an instant. His dreams and his home were buried along with him. He had scrimped and saved to furnish our home. He often proudly showed it off to his friends, reminiscing about the sacrifices he had made to provide for his family. He used to say, 'Life has been a journey, a long road I walked with rough hands and a tired heart. From my youth to now, I worked hard. But when I look back, I find comfort in knowing that my children and their children won't face the same struggles. The challenges I faced paved the way for their happiness and peaceful days in this home. I have no regrets, only a deep sense of contentment that trading my life for their well-being was a choice I'd make again without hesitation.'

It had only been two years since Zariya and I married, and she came to that house. Mama and Baba had no daughter, and I was their only son. Therefore, Mama had always longed for a daughter, and she found that wish fulfilled in Zariya. They showered her with affection, favoring her in every matter and often siding with her in our disagreements. Zariya was raised by her aunt after her parents tragically passed away in a bomb blast when she was just seven years old. Thus, Mama and Baba's love for her was not in vain; it was reciprocated in the most beautiful ways. I sometimes felt envious of Zariya because Baba had always been preoccupied with work since I was a child. I could only recall a few precious moments of sitting with him or talking to him about school or work. Yet, he would often go for walks with Zariya, take her shopping, bring her and Mama on every trip with him, and let her buy anything her heart desired. He would even bring her treats, just like the ones I got for Aleha. She was their favorite child and was more attached to them, spending more time with them than me; hence, her pain and devastation at their loss were undoubtedly greater than mine. Zariya had lost both sets of parents—the ones she was related to by blood and the ones she had grown close to in her heart.

"Rayan, I am tired. Can we sit for a while on the bench?" Zariya gently pressed my arm and looked into my eyes. Her brown, shiny eyes were darkened, and the glitter had been washed away from tears since Mama and Baba died. We were passing through a graveyard. I extended my arms across her shoulder and took her to sit on the bench. I put sleeping Aleha on her lap, sat beside her, and pulled her closer. We left the road long ago, and now we had just passed the thin ally and reached this place. It was a graveyard, and two benches were placed vertically on each side before the big metal gate at the front door of the graveyard under a tree. Zariya placed her head on my shoulder and stared inside the graveyard through the space between metal bars. One streak of tears soaked her face. I tightened my grip around. Every time I proposed to leave Syria and come to the UK, she refused, clinging to the hope of visiting Mama and Baba's graves when she yearned for their presence.

"Zariya, I'm so sorry for putting you and Aleha through all this. I didn't have any other choice, but I regret that it caused you pain."

She didn't respond, her gaze fixed on the graveyard.

"I refused to work in the warehouse, but you didn't say anything. I held your hand, but you walked out without a word."

"Rayan, the day I married you, I gave myself to you completely. You are my world. I will do whatever you ask without question. I have always believed you would do everything you could to make us happy."

Her face was expressionless, her eyes unmoving, and her voice heavy with sorrow. She stared at the graveyard without blinking. Remorse and guilt washed over me, and I couldn't bring myself to speak. I remained silent for the rest of the time.

"Rayan, no matter how hard we try, we can't escape death. If our time has come, it will come. Mama and Baba didn't expect to leave us so soon. They were healthy and happy." Her voice trembled as she took a deep breath.

"But... but... but they're right there," she said, lifting her hand and pointing to the graveyard. She looked at me, and another tear rolled down her face.

"Are we going to die too?" She sobbed for a few minutes, and I held her tightly as she buried her face in my chest.

"Nonsense," I reassured her. "We'll make it through this. I'll find a job, inshallah, and we'll rent a little house here. Everything will be okay. Just trust me, habibiti. Stop crying."

I gently patted her back, and her sobs gradually subsided. I tried to instill confidence in her, but deep down, I wasn't sure if we'd survive. The biting cold was seeping into my bones, and my body trembled. I knew we had to act quickly to find food and shelter before it was too late.

I rose to my feet and said, "I'll go look for some food. You stay here with Aleha."

Zariya shook her head vehemently, her eyes wide with fear. "I'm scared," she whispered, her vulnerability tugging at my heartstrings. "I am going with you."

"But you just said you were tired, didn't you?" I pointed it out.

"Yes, but..."

"Please," I pleaded. I sat beside her and gently clasped her soft, smooth hands in mine. Her touch was as delicate as silk. "It will only take an hour or two. Do you want us to starve? Huh? Tell me." She hesitated for a moment, her eyes pleading with me. "Then let me go. I promise I won't be long. Can I go now?" I asked gently.

She nodded slowly, her fear giving way to trust.

"Good girl," I murmured, patting her head affectionately.

CHAPTER 5

The cobblestone street buzzed with life, filled with laughter, talking, and the clanging of pots and pans. Bakeries wafted the delicious scent of fresh bread, couples enjoyed bowls of pasta together, and children giggled while eating ice cream cones. Two friends engaged in a lively conversation, savoring their hot coffees and their laughter filling the air. Even in the midst of all the activity, two students diligently worked on their homework, sharing the load as they enjoyed a pizza. This scene resonated with a memory of Yousef and me. Every Sunday, a familiar aroma of sizzling meat and roasting spices would draw us, like moths to a flame, to Uncle Hakim's Shwarma shop. Uncle Hakim, a rotund man with a handlebar mustache perpetually stained with paprika, would greet us with a booming laugh and a twinkle in his warm brown eyes. He knew each of our orders by heart, his calloused hands assembling our shwarma with lightning speed. The pita bread, still warm from the oven, cradles juicy, marinated chicken layered with crisp lettuce, tangy tomato, and creamy tahini sauce. Uncle Hakim, ever the generous host, always rewarded our loyalty with a conspiratorial wink and a 5% discount. The shops around me gave me a similar energy. The day's rush swept by, with some faces tired from work and others eagerly heading home. Men in suits hurried past, returning to their cozy nests filled with cherished belongings and comfortable beds for rest. There was a time when I had all of that, too. But did I appreciate it? No, my foolish heart yearned for more instead of being grateful. Why do we chase after what seems better, only to realize the true value of what we had when it's gone?

A few minutes later, I turned a corner and stumbled upon a different neighborhood. This one had a distinctly European vibe, but the people felt familiar. Some, in traditional clothing, reminded me of Pakistanis. My dad had worn similar clothes gifted by his friend Gul Sher after meeting at the '2010 Shaheed Benazir Bhutto International Boxing Tournament.' He called them Shalwar Kameez and wore them with pride.

Seeing shops and grocery stores with signs in Farsi, Arabic, and Urdu made the area feel more welcoming. An Arabic phone repair shop with a 'Help Wanted' sign offering the job to Arabic speakers caught my eye. This was my chance! I often visited my friend

Yousef at his phone repair shop. He'd taught me some basics, like assessing device damage, handling water exposure, and installing covers and screen protectors. I knew I could be helpful. Taking a deep breath, I walked in, ready to explain my situation. My wife and daughter needed food, and I hoped they'd understand, being fellow humans speaking the same language. Trusting their compassion, I summoned the courage to ask for the job.

Walking into the phone repair shop for the first time as an interviewee, I felt a knot of nerves in my stomach. I took a deep breath and pushed open the small door. Inside, the space was cramped, with a long counter and a display case showcasing different phone models. Behind the counter, a tired-looking cashier with a salt-and-pepper beard and tawny skin sat on a stool, dozing off. He wore a skullcap on his head. Nearby, two young men in their twenties were busy repairing phones. One had neatly combed side-parted hair and ocean-blue eyes, wearing a green hoodie. The other had a mischievous grin, dark brown curls resembling a sparrow's nest, and a crooked nose. He wore a black sweatshirt.

Approaching the first young man, I greeted him, "As-salaam 'alaykum."

He lifted his weary eyes, a flicker of surprise crossing his face. "Wa 'alaykum as-salaam," he responded, his tone neutral. "How can I help you?"

"My name is Rayan," I continued, stepping closer, "and I just arrived in the UK. I have no papers, no work, and no money to feed my family. I desperately need a job." My voice dipped, vulnerability creeping in. "Back home, at a friend's repair shop. I learned the basics, and I'm a fast learner; inshallah, I will learn the rest."

He held my gaze, his expression unreadable. A knot of fear tightened in my stomach—a fear unlike any I'd known before. The uncertainty of our future in this new country, the gnawing worry of rejection, the terror of being discovered as an undocumented immigrant... my mind painted a grim picture of police, jail, and life ripped apart. What would happen to Zariya and Aleha? Would they, too, be condemned to a prison existence? The weight of these anxieties weighed heavily, drying my throat, turning my palms clammy, and pinning my eyes to his face.

He glanced at me, his face a mixture of surprise and disapproval. Then, he approached another person and whispered something in their ear. With a furrowed brow, he quickly made his way to the storage room in the corner. Moments later, the first boy approached me with a stern expression and a deep voice that rumbled like distant thunder, saying, "You'll have to wait," his tone leaving no room for argument.

Sinking onto the maroon leather stool standing against the wall, I leaned my head against the cool wall. Uncertainty gnawed at me. What had just happened? What was coming next? My nervousness remained a prickly knot in my stomach, my inner voice whispering warnings. Fifteen minutes crawled by on the display case clock. Each tick hammered against my skull. Then came the wail of police sirens. It was like a punch to the gut—confirmation of my premonition.

My heart raced, and panic consumed my thoughts. All I could think about was escaping, running as fast as my trembling legs could carry me. Thoughts of Zariya and Aleha, their innocent faces filled with fear, flashed through my mind. I couldn't bear the thought of leaving them alone if I ended up in jail. Our carefully built life would crumble, and the looming threat of deportation haunted me. It felt like we would be thrown back into the nightmare we had fought so hard to escape. The pain and constant fear would consume us once again. We had sacrificed everything to break free from that life. Would it all be in vain? Was there no way to escape this cycle of fear and suffering? At that moment, the fear of being pursued paled in comparison to the fear of returning to a life of danger and despair. So, I made a choice—I ran. Amidst the chaos, all I could hear was the sound of my own hurried footsteps, stumbling and falling as I fled the store.

CHAPTER 6

Relief washed over me as the absence of sirens confirmed my safety. Satisfied I was far enough away, I hurried towards Zariya. But reaching the spot near the graveyard, where I'd left them, the ground vanished beneath my feet. The bench was empty. My heart hammered against my ribs, threatening to burst. Sweat trickled down my face, and my legs shook like leaves in a storm. A million terrifying thoughts bombarded me: Kidnapped? By whom? Why? Not for money, I have none. The Police? Did they get caught? Deported? Where would I even begin to look? My mind was on the verge of implosion, my lips about to scream their names. With unsteady steps, my legs failing me, I stumbled, fell, and then pushed myself back up, fuelled by a raw mix of fear, hunger, and exhaustion. Each step felt heavier than the last, but I pushed on, the weight of what might have happened pressing down on me, urging me forward in my desperate search. I walked, lost in a daze, as the unfamiliar streets blended together. Junctions, buildings, countless houses—I couldn't keep track of how many I had passed in my desperate search. My memory was a void, replaced by the pounding ache in my head and the relentless pain in my heart. With heavy steps, I pushed myself forward, my voice hoarse from calling out their names. I could feel unsympathetic eyes on me, perhaps unable to comprehend the weight of my despair. Eventually, my body reached its limit. Each step felt like an eternity, my head spinning, until the world faded into a blur of dim lights, and darkness took over.

The guilt overwhelmed me as I wished I had never left them alone. Zariya's image flashed before my eyes. Then, I wished I had never left my country. I remembered Yousef telling me not to go, but I was hurt and afraid. People might have thought I was wrong or cowardly, but my fear was not for myself; it was for my family. What I did was what a husband should do and what a father would have done, too. We had nothing left. Our home lay in ruins. With nowhere to go, my dreams crumbled further as my business closed down. We buried Mama and Baba, then joined other displaced families in a small, donated tent. It was cramped and uncomfortable, with barely enough space for two people. We couldn't afford bedding, so I found cardboard to lie on, but it offered little protection from the freezing cold floor. No matter how close we huddled, we couldn't find warmth. Each night felt like lying on ice, the cold seeping into our bones. In those dark moments, I couldn't help but wish to be reunited with Mama and Baba, even if it meant finding peace in the cold embrace of the grave. Anything seemed better than the bone-chilling reality we faced.

One day, Aunt Salama offered me refuge in her home, and I found myself hesitating. I had always heard negative things about her family. There were stories of a runaway daughter and a son with violent outbursts that landed his wife in the hospital and led to divorce. I couldn't help but wonder, What kind of man hurts his wife? It appalled me to even think about it. How could anyone claim bravery by oppressing the weaker one? The mere thought disgusted me. And then there was the son with addiction, repeatedly caught up in the justice system. These stories fueled my apprehension, and the idea of freezing on the streets seemed preferable to entering that household. But as I contemplated my decision, it became clear that it wasn't just my life at stake. The futures of Zariya and Aleha weighed heavily on my mind. Could I risk their safety for the sake of my own pride? This decision wasn't solely mine to make.

Her house was a three-bedroom apartment that lacked vibrancy. As you entered, you'd notice a hallway adorned with black wallpaper and silver lining. In the living room, was a sleek black leather sofa facing an LCD television, accompanied by a dining table elegantly set with a black tablecloth and silver runner. Six chairs surrounded the table, inviting guests to sit and dine comfortably. Aunt Salama kindly offered us her daughter's room. Stepping inside, the air felt heavy with bittersweet memories and unspoken emotions. The small room was bathed in a soft, warm glow from the afternoon sun filtering through the window. The faded pink wallpaper held onto whispers of childhood laughter. A bed with a tall, ornately carved headboard dominated the space, adorned with a neatly folded, mismatched quilt. Above the headboard hung a large portrait of her daughter. This small room was our safe place for a while.

The atmosphere in the house grew increasingly tense as Zariya spent more time alone with Aunt Salama. Nabil, her eldest son, took on the role of the sole breadwinner after Uncle Jamal's passing. However, he seemed distant and withdrawn, often absent from home due to his late work schedule. Aunt Salama brushed off any questions about his work, leaving us to wonder about the true nature of his absence. It became clear that Aunt Salama played a larger role in the family's issues when we observed Jabal, her drug-addicted son, spiraling out of control with a narcissistic and rude attitude. To avoid him, we mostly stayed in our room, only encountering him during uncomfortable meals. His once polite inquiries about our day had turned into grunts and brief responses before he would abruptly leave, his face filled with annoyance. One evening, while watching TV, Aunt Salama suggested a family picnic, but Jabal scoffed at the idea, questioning why we would waste time with people we barely knew. His dismissive tone made us feel unwelcome and unwanted. Despite Aunt Salama's dismissal of Jabal's behavior, attributing it to his usual gruffness, we couldn't ignore the growing tension and unease. As weeks passed, his actions became more aggressive, slamming doors and creating an oppressive atmosphere that seemed to surround us like an inescapable fog.

One Saturday afternoon, The sun was shining through the windows, casting long shadows in Aunt Salama's apartment. Aunt Salama had some errands to run, so she left. Shortly after, Uncle Jamal called me. He told me that his son, who I considered like a brother, was tragically killed in a shooting last week. I went out to meet Uncle Jamal and offer my condolences. It was a heartbreaking moment. Zariya being alone with Jabal was a constant worry that haunted me every step of the way. When I returned, the silence was shattered by a piercing scream that cut through the air like a sharp blade. Panic gripped my throat as I sprinted up the stairs, each heavy footfall echoing my growing fear. I pounded on the door, my knuckles screaming Zariya's name until they throbbed. The door creaked open, revealing a tearful Zariya, her tiny body trembling as she clung to me tightly. Behind her, Jabal stood, his face twisted in rage, a glint of steel in his hand. The air crackled with unspoken threats, the knife chillingly punctuating his silence.

Later, after Jabal left and Aunt Salama returned, we shared the terrifying experience. She dismissed it quickly, waving it away as just a bad day for Jabal, attributing his outburst to drugs. "He wouldn't hurt a fly; we're family, after all," she sighed.

But her words held no solace. This wasn't a bad day; it was a glimpse into a darkness I refused to ignore. "We can't stay here," I whispered, the words heavy with conviction. A plan, fueled by fear and a desperate need to protect, began to form in my mind. Aunt Salama might have chosen to ignore the darkness, but I wouldn't. We had to leave, and fast.

CHAPTER 7

I awoke with a throbbing ache in my left side. Blood dripped from my forehead down my face, and my head felt heavy, a suffocating weight on my chest. Pushing myself up with trembling hands, I lifted my aching body off the cold ground. I was sprawled in bushes beside the sidewalk. Sun was just rising, painting the sky a soft yellow, but I felt no warmth. All I felt was the icy grip of fear. Memories of Zariya and Aleha flooded my mind like a dam bursting. With desperate hope, I stumbled towards the place I left them yesterday, each step fuelled by the gnawing fear of what I would do if I didn't find them. My heart kept leading me back there, whispering that where you lose something is often where you find it again. But when I reached the spot, it was empty. My heart crumbled once more, shattering the fragile hope that had kept me going. Exhausted and defeated, I stood there. Would I ever see my Aleha and Zariya again? Suddenly, a hand touched my shoulder. A jolt of adrenaline shot through me, followed by a surge of recognition. How could I forget that familiar touch? I spun around, my heart leaping into my throat. Zariya stood there, tears streaming down her face like a broken dam. Aleha clung to her chest, whimpering softly.

"Where were you?" Zariya cried, her voice thick with fear and anger. "I waited all night! We could have been..." she choked on a sob, the unspoken threat hanging heavy in the air. "How could you do this? How dare you!" Her voice broke, laced with hurt and betrayal. "I hate you! I never want to speak to you again!" She took a shaky breath, but before she could continue, I met her gaze, my eyes brimming with tears. My voice cracked as I whispered, "I'm so sorry."

No words could capture the intensity of our emotions at that moment. We leaned against each other, tears streaming down our faces. We didn't need words to understand the pain, regret, and relief we felt. The silence spoke volumes.

CHAPTER 8

"Take a bite," I offered, reaching out the burger I'd been given at the charity stall feeding the homeless. "I'm starving. Have it before it gets cold."

"I'm not hungry," Zariya said, pushing the burger away. "But you haven't eaten anything, and it's been thirty-six hours now. Have it. Otherwise, you'll pass out."

"No, I don't want it," she insisted.

"Okay, then," I sighed, placing both boxes back in our bag. "Come on, let's go find somewhere to rest."

"Why haven't you eaten your burger?" she asked suddenly.

"I'm not hungry either," I replied.

"But you just said you were starving..."

"Yes, I was," I admitted. "But I'm not anymore."

She eyed me skeptically for a moment before nodding. "Okay, fine. Let's move."

"No, wait," she said, surprising me. "We'll eat first. I'm hungry now."

I sat down and took the boxes of burgers out of the bag, then opened them and handed one to her. I didn't ask her any questions; I knew she was angry and annoyed with me, and her refusal to eat was her way of expressing her anger and protest. However, today, she seemed to lack the energy for such a display, and she didn't want me to go hungry. We ate in silence and then continued on to find a place to rest.

As we walked along the city streets, we were struck by the bustling crowd hurrying about their busy lives, the double-decker buses, and the beautiful buildings and skyscrapers. Eventually, we turned onto a quieter road. Suddenly, I heard the sound of a siren, and the events of yesterday flashed before my eyes. I immediately grabbed Zariya's hand and led her down a narrow street to hide. Two ambulances rushed by.

"Oh, thank God it's an ambulance! I thought it was the police," I said with relief.

We emerged from our hiding place and continued walking on the street. The cold bit into our skin, making us shiver. My mind raced with worries about our future in this city.

"Why... What happened?" Zariya asked innocently.

I had no answer. I was searching for one myself. Shame washed over me, making me look away from her accusing eyes. I couldn't lie, so I remained silent, pretending not to hear. But burying your head in the sand doesn't make problems disappear.

"Rayan, you haven't answered my question," she said, her voice firm this time.

I knew I couldn't avoid it any longer. "What? I'm sorry, I wasn't listening..." I stammered.

"Are we going to live like this forever? Hiding in fear?" she asked, her voice filled with pain. "Is this why we came here? We can't even breathe freely in this country!

I was supposed to be her pillar of strength, but I couldn't tell her the truth. The truth is that I regretted our decision. That maybe she was right—dying with dignity in our homeland was better than playing hide and seek with police here. But I couldn't let her lose hope.

Life is about sacrifice," I said, forcing a smile. "We've made a big sacrifice, but the rewards will be great. We are facing some problems, but trust me, these problems will not persist for long. When the night gets darker, it means that the sun is going to rise. The sun of our luck and betterment will rise, too."

Her eyes searched mine, filled with a hopeful glint. "Did you get any job?"

I swallowed, debating between truth and comfort. "Not yet, Zariya. I stopped by a few shops, and they said they'd keep me in mind... but there weren't any openings right now."

The guilt gnawed at me. I couldn't help but remember the scolding I received from Baba when I lied about not pushing Bilal in the cycle race when I was five. He reminded me that even if no one else saw, Allah did. "I did not see you, so you may escape my punishment but fear the punishment of Al-Baseer, the One who sees all," he said.

I squeezed my eyes shut, seeking forgiveness. "Forgive me, Lord, You are Al-Aleem," I whispered, "You are All-Knowing. Forgive me for lying to my wife. You know my struggle, my fear for her sake."

When I opened my eyes, Zariya was still looking at me, her expression unreadable. "Don´t worry, we'll keep trying, Insha'Allah. We have each other, and that's what matters most."

We finally arrived at a bustling street filled with life and energy. Refugees had made the sidewalks their temporary homes. At one end, a group of four people were deeply engrossed in a card game, surrounded by laughter and smoke. On the opposite side sat an elderly man with a long white beard and hair, his face partially hidden. Before him, there was an empty vase. Intrigued by his serene presence, we settled near his small shelter, closer to him than the lively card game. Unbeknownst to us, we were within earshot of his attentive gaze. As we looked around, we saw other families and groups scattered across the pavement.

For now, we had no choice but to stay there. Finding a decent place to live felt like a distant dream. "Are you okay?" I asked, concern lacing my voice.

She met my gaze, a small smile playing on her lips. "Yes, I'll be alright," she said, rubbing her left arm with her right hand.

The lie hung heavy in the air. It wasn't lost on me. "Actually, you're not," I countered gently. "Here, take my jacket." I draped it over her shoulders, the thin fabric offering meager protection against the encroaching chill.

"What about you?" she asked, worry flickering in her eyes.

"Don't worry," I chuckled, feigning warmth despite the goosebumps erupting on my skin. "I'm actually warm, see?" I gestured to my forehead and neck, beads of sweat forming there. But it wasn't sweat, not entirely. Earlier, it had been drizzling, and a few stray droplets lingered on my forehead, trailing down my neck.

With weary smiles, she leaned against the wall, seeking solace in exhaustion. I took Aleha off her lap and kept her entertained while hoping for a momentary reprieve; she closed her eyes.

CHAPTER 9

Laughter echoed through the air as I played with Aleha, giving Zariya a well-deserved break. Little fingers tugged at my growing beard, sweet kisses landed on my nose, and she playfully nibbled on my finger before drifting off to sleep, her giggles fading into soft snores. Exhaustion soon overtook me, and we both fell into a deep slumber. However, our peaceful rest was abruptly interrupted by Aleha's cries. I tried to soothe her quietly, aware that Zariya wouldn't appreciate a serenade. But despite my efforts to rock, sway, and shush, her cries only grew louder. Desperate, I carried her through the calm streets, hoping a change of scenery would work its magic. Yet, when we returned to our temporary shelter, the storm of her cries remained. Finally, I gently woke Zariya up.

"Hungry, maybe?" I suggested, my voice raspy with fatigue.

Zariya nodded, rummaging through our meager supplies. Soon, a bottle of milk was in Aleha's tiny hands. The cries subsided, replaced by contented gurgles. Finally, with a sleepy sigh, she drifted back to sleep. My stomach rumbled in agreement. "Me too," I mumbled, "and probably you too." A wave of determination washed over me.

"Don't worry," I whispered to Zariya, "I'll find something, anything. Just stay put, okay?"

I set off for the night. My mind raced, searching for any opportunity, any kind of work that could feed my family. The job hunt was on again.

Night fell, and my mind raced like a hamster on a wheel. Every corner I turned, every shop window I peeked into, hope flickered for a job, any job, to feed my family. I drifted through the town center, searching for that magic 'Help Wanted' sign. One shop, two shops, each vacancy board felt like a slap in the face. Gathering my courage, I mumbled the question I knew the answer to: "Openings?"

The reply was predictable, a shake of the head and a closed-off smile. Walking on, I watched families pass, faces lit by the warm glow of streetlights. A couple shared ice cream, their child running ahead, carefree. A man held his father's hand, their quiet conversation speaking volumes. I felt a pang, not just for myself but for everyone back home. Here, life moved with a rhythm of normalcy. No fear of sirens, no whispers of war. Children dreamt of futures filled with possibilities, not the chilling reality of loss. Back home, children played with the weight of grief, lifting pieces of their parents and their bodies instead of toys.

I didn't give up. My feet pounded the pavement, searching for 'Help Wanted' signs until even the last shop flickered to black. Returning back and telling Zariya the truth felt impossible. When I got back, she asked if I had found work.

"Not today," I mumbled, pasting on a smile.

"There's always hope, right?" she asked, her eyes searching mine for reassurance, a lifeline in the face of their harsh reality.

"Of course," I declared, my voice echoing hollowly despite its strength. My stomach churned with guilt. "I'm so sorry I couldn't find anything for us to eat," I whispered.

Zariya turned away, her tiny body curled inwards. "I'm not hungry," she mumbled, but I could hear the tremor in her voice. Silence filled the small space, broken only by the rumble of my own stomach. I lay beside her, closing my eyes, trying to ignore the gnawing emptiness.

Suddenly, a raspy voice startled me. I looked up to see the old man from the next bunk holding out a small plastic box. He gestured towards it, his eyes filled with concern.

Zariya stirred and sat up, her gaze shifting between me and the box.

"No, no, it's fine," I stammered, pushing the box back gently. "You keep it."

The old man persisted, a determined glint in his eyes. With a gentle force, he placed the box in my hand before shuffling away.

"What was he saying?" Zariya asked, her voice laced with curiosity.

"I don't know, sweetheart," I admitted. "He might be mute."

She frowned, her expression clouded with sadness. "That's so unfortunate," she sighed.

I squeezed her hand. "Maybe," I began, trying to find the right words, "when God takes away one of our senses, he strengthens the others to compensate. Like, maybe he has incredible hearing or a really good sense of smell."

Her eyes brightened slightly. "What did he give you?"

I opened the box, revealing two neatly halved burgers and a handful of fries. My mouth watered, but I knew what I had to do.

"Here," I said, offering the box to Zariya. "Eat this."

She shook her head stubbornly. "No, you eat first."

"Zariya, please," I insisted, a hint of sternness in my voice. "Don't be stubborn. We both need it."

She remained silent, her jaw set. My frustration mounted, but I knew a fight wouldn't help.

"Alright," I sighed, taking a large bite of the burger. "See? It's good. Now share with me."

This time, she didn't argue. Slowly, she reached for the box, a small smile playing on her lips. As we ate, the silence was no longer filled with emptiness but with the soft crunch of fries and the quiet murmur of our shared meal. The gesture of the old man, even though we couldn't understand his words, spoke volumes, reminding us that kindness and compassion can transcend any barrier.

CHAPTER 10

The loud noise of street cleaners abruptly woke me up, causing me to cough. I noticed blankets covering us, but I wasn't sure where they came from. Zariyah snuggled beside me and was cozily wrapped in one of them. The old man beside us was sleeping without a blanket, confirming my suspicion that he had given it to us last night. This small act of kindness sparked a glimmer of hope inside me. However, my hope quickly faded as I saw a newspaper scrap flying by with a headline that hit me hard: 'Home Minister Says: No Illegals! Crackdown Intensifies.' The images of handcuffed people and clashes with the police mirrored the fear that was swirling in my stomach. Each word shattered my hope, like dry leaves crumbling away.

"Where did the blankets come from?" Zariyah's voice, raw with sleep, startled me. "I think they're the old man's," I whispered, relieved she hadn't seen the news.

I scrambled the paper and put it in my pocket. Shame burned my throat. How could I thank him enough, not just for this, but for his kindness yesterday?

I stood up, took the blanket with me, and walked towards him. He stirred as I laid the blanket back over him. His wrinkled eyes crinkled in a warm smile. "Thank you," I signed, my voice tight.

He sat down and shook his head slightly. I grasped his hand; his calloused fingers were surprisingly strong. "You are a good man. My name is Rayan. If you need help, I would love help," I said reassuringly, But I had nothing to offer. I had no money, no warm clothes, and nothing to eat to give back his favor, but I promised myself. When things got better, I couldn't repay him, but I tried to repay him.

Zariyah's cry shattered the tense silence between us. "Rayan!" she sobbed. "Aleha's burning up!"

I rushed towards her, my heart pounding with panic, fueled by the troubling news I had heard. But I refused to let myself crumble. Not now. I sat down beside her, cradling the warm, burning body of Aleha in my lap. Her eyes were closed, her brow furrowed in discomfort, and each shallow breath seemed like a struggle. How could I have forgotten about Aleha? I felt ashamed as a father. I knew I had to take her to the doctor.

How could I ease her suffering when I felt so powerless? If only I could absorb her fever, take her pain upon myself. But wishing wouldn't heal her. I had to be strong, not just for her but for Zariyah, for the glimmer of hope that refused to be extinguished. "Don't worry," I rasped despite the frantic hammering of my heart. "It's just a fever. We'll figure something out. We have to."

But how? My mind raced, trapped in a maze of fear and desperation. Had we crossed oceans and risked everything, only to die here? I gently planted a kiss on Aleha's warm forehead, tasting the tang of fear on my tongue. Her feverish skin tingled against mine, and her shallow breaths struggled to fill her lungs. Tears welled up in my eyes, ready to spill over, but I held them back, refusing to let despair consume me. Giving up was never an option. For their future, for the life we still dared to dream of, I would find a way. Even if it meant moving mountains, I would search for a doctor, seek out medicine, and do whatever it took to bring back the sparkle in her feverish eyes.

CHAPTER 11

My visit to Uncle Jamal's house was intended to offer condolences for his son's loss but soon turned into a conversation about our own family's struggles. He and Baba, childhood friends and legal partners since the 1980s, ran their consultancy firm on King Faisal Street in Aleppo. However, after Baba's passing, Uncle Jamal's health declined, forcing him to sell the firm. Despite the meager proceeds due to the turbulent times, he generously shared some with me, even offering me a place to stay in his house.

Since his wife's passing, the Uncle had been alone, and recently, his only son was killed as well. His only remaining connection, his daughter Layla, lived a world away in the UK. She'd built a life with a husband and children he barely knew, having gone there to study, fallen in love with an Englishman, and settled down far away. He disapproved of her marriage, distancing them further. Now, alone in a crumbling city, he yearned for her anchor.

While at his house, I met Abdel, son of his and Baba's other partner, Mahmoud. Mahmoud's death just months into working with them. The opposing party he'd won a case against had silenced him forever. I recalled Mama's pleas for security, echoing against Baba's unwavering faith. He said, "I will only die when Allah wills. Nobody can harm me only when it is written by Him." Yet, fate seemed to have turned its back on Aleppo. Abdel, his voice laced with despair, spoke of sending his family to the US. It mirrored the ache in my own heart. Gave some contacts of the agents that helped me leave the country.

CHAPTER 12

Resting my head against the rough wall, I desperately searched for answers. Every touch to Aleha's forehead was a prayer for her fever to break. But her temperature remained, stealing hope from my grasp. My heart raced with her fever, pounding in my chest. Uncle Jamal's vacant eyes haunted me, reminding me of the pain he felt after losing his son. I remembered nights by his side, with Zariyah and me flanking his bed. He would tell stories of love, his marriage, and the joy of Layla's birth. Then, his son Sameer, a brilliant boy destined to be a doctor. But in an instant, Sameer was gone, shattering Uncle Jamal's world. Now, holding Aleha close, I felt the weight of Uncle Jamal's pain. Watching your child wither, their flame dimmed, is a burden heavier than any stone. I saw it in his eyes, the emptiness left by a loss too deep to heal. He buried his young son, a vibrant child full of life, stolen away by fate. The pride he felt watching Sameer pursue his dream of becoming a doctor turned to ashes. To see your child so fragile, battling an unseen enemy, is a fear that claws at your soul.

One day, an airstrike ripped through our neighborhood. In minutes, a building near us crumbled into dust. We fled once again, refugees with nowhere to turn. We found ourselves outside Aleppo, huddled in a camp for displaced people. The dust-choked air of the camp carried with it the scent of despair and desperation. Tents stretched as far as the eye could see, each one a fragile shelter against biting cold nights.

The health of Uncle Jamal started to deteriorate. Grief for his lost son had sapped his strength, leaving him vulnerable to the harsh realities of the camp. Zariya, her own heart heavy with loss, tried her best. She'd gather scarce scraps of food, coaxing him to eat with stories of his wife and children. One night, a particularly biting wind swept through the camp, carrying with it the chill of despair. Uncle Jamal, whose body was already weakened by grief and illness, succumbed. His cough, ragged and weak for weeks, turned into a final rasp, leaving behind a silence heavier than the dust that choked the camp.

Zariya was very unsettled by Uncle Jamal's death, the hollowness in her eyes mirroring the emptiness in her heart. She missed Uncle Jamal's gentle hand resting on hers, his stories whispered in the quiet of the night.

The lack of proper medical care likely played a significant role in Uncle Jamal's death. The camp clinic, overwhelmed and under-resourced, could offer little beyond basic treatments. His weakened state, coupled with malnutrition, had made him susceptible to even minor infections or complications. Witnessing Uncle Jamal's decline and his slow surrender to the harsh realities of the camp had taken a heavy toll on Zariyah. The loss of not just her father figure but also a confidant and friend left her feeling utterly alone.

CHAPTER 13

Tremor ran through my voice as I spoke into the receiver. "Is this Sister Layla?"

Relief tinged the voice on the other end. "Yes, it is. Who's speaking?"

My chest tightened. "It's Rayan Mustafa, son of Shams Mustafa, Uncle Jamal's friend and business partner." The cold coins in my hand, from the kind old man, seemed to absorb my nervousness.

A flicker of surprise. "Shams uncle! I know him well. How can I help you, Rayan? And how did you get my number?"

Shame tinged my apology. "I'm so sorry, but Uncle Jamal told me to call you before... everything happened. Your number was still in my phone." I poured out the story, my voice thick with emotion, not hesitating to share the hardship and the loss. I could feel the weight of silence hanging in the air after Layla's soft promise, "I'll be there." The words echoed in my ears as I guided her through the directions, knowing she would arrive in six hours. As I broke the news of Uncle Jamal's passing, the phone line fell silent for what seemed like an eternity. Ten long minutes filled only with the sound of her muffled sobs. It had been years since they had spoken; ever since her marriage, Uncle Jamal would ignore her calls. But the day before we had to evacuate, Zariya and I managed to convince him to reach out. I dialed Layla's number, hoping for a connection, but she missed the call. Then, the chaos of evacuation engulfed us, and everything else became a blur of survival. Uncle Jamal never got the chance to truly reconcile with his daughter. Layla, though, possessed the same kindness that radiated from Uncle Jamal's face whenever I poured out our troubles. She listened with patience, empathy, and unwavering support. In her voice, I could hear the same warmth Uncle Jamal had always spoken of. He had raised an extraordinary woman, and as I spoke, I understood why he spoke of her with such pride.

CHAPTER 14

I hung up the receiver and stepped out of the phone booth, taking in the sight of the ominous sky above. Oppressive clouds cast a leaden blanket over the sky. Since arriving here, we hadn't seen a glimpse of the sun, only felt the incessant drumming of raindrops. But today, the weather took a turn for the worse. It was only 5:00 p.m., yet the darkness enveloped the surroundings, resembling the depths of a midnight hour. The clouds gathered ominously, ready to unleash a torrential rain that would drench everything in its path. The lightning crackled fiercely, its intensity threatening to wreak havoc. Slowly, I trudged back to our shelter. Six agonizing hours stretched before us, with every passing second reminding me of Aleha's worsening condition. It was Zariyah who remembered Uncle Jamal's daughter living in the UK. We scrambled through my phone, fingers flying across the screen. After half an hour, her number materialized like a beacon of hope.

Talking about Layla always stirred up intense emotions in Uncle Jamal. It would choke him up and make his voice tremble. Layla, unlike her spirited brother, was an obedient child who followed his every word. He took great pride in her compliance. But when she moved to the UK for medical studies, the obedient daughter disappeared, replaced by a fiery Layla who questioned, argued, and even defied him by marrying a man he considered unsuitable. He described this man with a trembling voice—a drinker, a smoker, maybe even worse. Despite his disapproval, Layla stood firm, leaving a void in Uncle Jamal's heart. He was torn between his love for her and his own pride. He shed tears, his heart ached, but his ego prevented him from reaching out. And when his ego finally crumbled, life dealt him a cruel blow, denying him any chance of reconciliation.

As I made a left turn, the noise of the roundabout faded away. The street ahead, leading to the bridge, was bustling with heavy traffic. People hurried home under the threatening sky as if anticipating the upcoming storm. Above, a group of birds gracefully danced in the sky, like an aerial ballet foreshadowing the approaching tempest. But inside me, the turmoil had calmed down to a gentle breeze. Talking to Layla had brought me immense relief, like a soothing ointment.

Only a few meters remained, with two traffic signals standing as sentinels before I could reach Zariya and Aleha. The uncertainty of how Layla would react and if she would lend us a hand weighed heavily on me, especially knowing that Aleha's life depended on it. But when she assured me she was on her way to help, a spark of hope ignited within me. Maybe Aleha would recover, my daughter would be safe, and our future would take a turn for the better. I passed the first pedestrian signal. The storm was close. I raised my head up, and the first fat raindrop splattered on my cheek, sending chills down my body. People around me were already taking out their umbrellas or covering their heads with jacket hoods. The familiar bite of winter felt different today, laced with an unspoken sadness that resonated within the depths of my being. I reached the last signal. I slammed my fist against the button. Fear tightened its icy grip around my heart as I saw the swarm of people at the crosswalk. My feet twitched with the urge to move forward, but anxiety, a serpent coiling tightly around my ankles, held me back. Every car that roared past felt like a near miss. Each close call sent a jolt of electricity through my body, leaving a trail of shivers in its wake.

I couldn't stay frozen. Taking a deep, shuddering breath that did little to calm the storm within, I lunged into the crosswalk. The world blurred into a cacophony of honking horns, screeching tires, and the frantic shouts of pedestrians. Adrenaline surged through my veins, fuelling my desperate movements. A car screeched to a halt mere inches from my outstretched hand, the driver's enraged face contorted in a mask of fury. His shouts were lost in the wind, swallowed by the symphony of the relentless storm. My eyes, wide with a mixture of fear and determination, remained glued to the other side of the road. Each agonizing step felt like an eternity, my breaths coming in shallow gasps that tore at my dry throat. Finally, after what felt like an hour, the light changed, signaling my chance to cross. Relief washed over me in a wave, momentary and fragile but enough to fuel my final push. Reaching the other side, I pushed through the crowd, my heart pounding a frantic tattoo against my ribs. Then I saw her, Zariya, her anguished cries piercing the air, clutching Aleha tightly to her chest. My throat tightened, a silent scream trapped within me.

CHAPTER 15

The rain was lashing down, the heaviest I had ever seen. The sky was weeping, mirroring the torrent of tears within me. My precious daughter clutched to my chest, usually light as a feather, now felt like a weight I could barely carry. Each step was a struggle, not only against her weight but against the crushing burden of grief. It was the weight of memories, our shared moments and laughter, now lost forever. As visions of happier times flooded my mind, tears streamed down my face, blurring the world around me. Thoughts of the anguish she must have endured before giving up made my heart turn to ice. If only I could rewind time. I would shower her with every comfort imaginable: a snug bed to chase away the cold nights, a world of toys to spark her laughter and endless games that would see us through the brightest days. I would cherish every touch, every kiss, every playful tug that brought a smile to her face.

Now, standing before the same graveyard in front of which we once sat together when Aleha was alive, a wave of crushing regrets washes over me. If I could have held her closer, protected her further. The thought of her absence leaves a gaping hole in my heart, a void filled with the echoes of 'what ifs' and 'I wish I had.'

The rain poured down, each drop like a drumbeat on the old tombstones. The air was heavy with the smell of wet earth, and there was a deep silence, broken only by the mournful sigh of the wind. I walked through the gate, and in my arms, I held my precious burden. With shaky hands, I gently laid them to rest beneath the shelter of a weeping willow, its branches dripping tears in understanding. Taking a trembling breath, I fought back the tears that threatened to spill. Leaving them for a moment, I trudged towards a small hut at the edge of the graveyard. Inside, a worn shovel hung on a nail, its handle smooth from countless touches. A sob escaped my lips, and tears streamed down my face, blurring my surroundings. Returning to the tree, I began the solemn task. With each dig of the shovel, a lifetime of memories played out before my eyes.

With a final thud of earth against wood, I stood there, my body a hollow shell, my heart a leaden weight. My breath rasped in my throat, each inhale a battle against the crushing grief that threatened to consume me whole. Tears long fought back finally spilled over, carving hot tracks down my face. My hands trembled as I reached out, gently placing her on the fresh mound of earth. Silence, thick and heavy, pressed down on me. The only sound was the ragged rhythm of my sobs. I knelt beside the grave, my body wracked with uncontrollable tremors. At that moment, I yearned to join her, to find solace in the embrace of the earth, to escape the unbearable pain of this empty world.

With a shaky breath, I rose to my feet. The journey ahead would be long and arduous, but I would carry her memory with me. As the sun dipped below the horizon, painting the sky in hues of orange and purple, I knew I had to go now before anyone could catch me. I whispered a silent promise: "I will never forget you, my Aleha."

CHAPTER 16

The chill night air bit at my skin as I returned to find Zariya slumped against the wall, her eyes closed in exhaustion. I sat beside her, gently stroking her cheek, chilled and flushed from the relentless cold. Her face was drawn and thin, her laughter lines etched with sorrow that seemed to have stained her soul. Each tear she'd cried for our lost Aleha left another mark of darkness. My mind refused to forget the image of her clawing at me, begging to keep our child. Blame welled up within me, a bitter tide against the forces that destroyed our home and tore us from all we knew. We have lost everything. How quickly the winds of fate have shifted against us, leaving us with nothing but each other. How uncertain life is! Once, our home overflowed with laughter— Mama, Baba, Zariya, Aleha, and I. Never did I imagine a day when I'd be huddled on a roadside in a foreign city, our family shattered, our home a distant memory.

Exhausted, I drifted off to sleep, haunted by fragmented memories of Aleha, arguments, accusations, and the agonizing weight of blame. The blaring horns of cars and the wail of sirens jolted me awake. I rubbed the sleep from my eyes and stood up to see what happened. A colossal traffic jam stretched as far as the first traffic light. Anxious faces peered from car windows, waiting for traffic to move forward. It seemed likely an accident had caused the congestion.

Wearily, I slumped back against the wall, my eyelids heavy as if weighed down by lead. Each passing hour blurred into the next, a heavy fatigue clouding my mind. My stomach rumbled, a harsh reminder that it had been well over a day since we ate half a stale burger. Hunger gnawed at me, but the thought of Zariya quickly overshadowed it. She needed food.

A surge of panic clawed at my throat. I needed to find work, or at least some food, for her. This wasn't a place to simply wait; the time was unknown. More than six hours must have passed since I called Layla. I needed to check in to see if she had any news. My hand instinctively reached out for Zariya, but the space beside me was empty. My heart lurched in my chest. Panic twisted my insides into a knot. Where could Zariya have gone? My mind raced a frantic search engine with no results. Had she wandered off, confused or disoriented? The thought sparked a surge of adrenaline. Without a second thought, I scrambled to my feet.

My legs, stiff from sleep and inactivity, protested in a dull ache, but I ignored them. I couldn't stay here, not a moment longer. I scanned the immediate area, my eyes darting from face to face, searching for a glimpse of Zariya's familiar form. My voice, hoarse from disuse, called her name: "Zariya! Zariya, where are you?" But there was no answer, only the cacophony of the city—the blaring horns, the distant sirens, the murmur of worried voices. My stomach churned with a sickening dread. The possibility I'd tried to ignore earlier, the one that had gnawed at the edges of my consciousness, now roared to the forefront of my mind. What if the accident, the one that caused the traffic jam, had happened near here?

Driven by this horrifying thought, I stumbled towards the scene of the congestion. A crowd had gathered at the edges, their faces etched with concern and curiosity.

Pushing through the throng, I jostled shoulders and muttered apologies. My voice, raw with desperation, rose above the din: "Excuse me, please! Has anyone seen a young woman?

Most people simply shook their heads, their gazes fixated on the scene before them. Frustration bubbled within me, a bitter counterpoint to the terror that threatened to consume me whole. Then, a glimmer of hope. A woman, her face etched with worry, spoke up. "There is a young woman…" Her voice trailed off, then she pointed towards Zariya lying on the floor. Her forehead was bleeding, a trickle running down her face. A man knelt beside her, his voice shaking as he asked, "Are you okay? Should I call an ambulance?"

I hurried towards Zariya. I reached her side and pulled her into a hug. "Zariya!" I exclaimed. I knew taking her to the hospital was risky, but her injuries demanded attention. "This is my wife," I explained to the concerned man. We need to get her out of here before the police arrive.

She leaned on me as we made our way back to our shelter. I examined her injuries more closely. Her forehead was bruised, and a small cut bled sluggishly. Her knees were scraped raw, and her twisted ankle was clearly swollen. I tore a strip of fabric from an old shirt and pressed it against the wound on her forehead, hoping to staunch the bleeding.

Just then, a black VW screeched to a halt in front of our building. As traffic thinned, a woman emerged, her steps purposeful. Dressed in white sneakers, a long black coat, and a pink and black scarf, her dark hair was pulled back in a neat bun. She slammed the car door shut and approached us.

"Sorry I'm late," she said with a smile that didn't quite reach her eyes.

"Layla?"

"Yes, it's me," she confirmed. "You must be Rayyan. I knew it the moment I saw you. Is this your wife? What happened to her? Why is she bleeding?"

"She had a minor accident," I replied curtly.

"Get in the car," Layla said, her voice laced with concern.

CHAPTER 17

Layla's house may have been small, but it had a warm and welcoming vibe. When you walked in, there were stairs on the left, and straight ahead was a cozy living room. There was a dining table near the entrance and two big couches with a glass coffee table in between. On the wall opposite the couches, there was a huge TV. Above it, Layla proudly displayed her medals, trophies, and photos with her adorable ten-year-old daughter. I plopped down on the couch, feeling much better than before. My headache had eased, but my stomach was rumbling with hunger. Layla had given us some fruit during the ride, but they were not sufficient to calm the hunger. I was so exhausted that I could barely keep my eyes open. I practically collapsed onto the couch, resting my head on the armrest.

Looking back, it was hard not to feel a sense of sadness. The conditions in the camps deteriorated rapidly after Uncle Jamal's passing. Zariya's health suffered, and the overall situation became dire. The camps were overcrowded, with tents bursting at the seams. There was a severe shortage of food and basic necessities. At first, the agent said that without any money he couldn´t help us. But a few days later, he called back with a risky plan. He said he could get us to England in a dangerous way and even find us a job. I didn't know what to do, so I talked to Yousef.

"Don't even think about it," Yousef said real seriously. "The agent is lying. You don't even know how dangerous it is. If you just want to die, stay here. At least you'll be home, where we can bury you properly. Don't risk getting lost at sea or eaten by wild animals."

Yousef's words hit me hard. When I got back to Zariya, I found her in a wretched state, her body wracked with fever and chills. The cold and dirt in the camps made her sick. There was no hope here. Half the city was destroyed, and even the camps were awful. Stuck with nowhere to go, I decided to take the agent's chance. It might be dangerous, but it had to be better than staying here for sure.

CHAPTER 18

My train of thought was interrupted when Layla entered. She cleared her throat to announce her presence. I immediately sat up, and she joined me on the sofa, placing a bowl of pasta on the coffee table.

"Sorry, I haven't cooked anything tonight. I made pasta for my daughter, and there were some leftovers in the fridge. I've ordered some more that will be here soon. In the meantime, have some pasta."

"Give it to Zariya," I suggested. "She might be hungry."

She smiled. "I really appreciate your concern for her, but I already gave her something to eat, and she's resting. She's probably asleep by now."

"Is she alright?" I asked.

"I cleaned her wounds," Layla explained. "She had some cuts on her knees and scratches on her hands, elbows, and forehead. I think these wounds will heal, but Rayyan, what I'm about to say might be difficult to hear. You need to get Zariya to see a psychiatrist.

The things that have happened to you both lately have caused her to slip into depression. You shouldn't take the risk of not going to a doctor. Her condition will only worsen otherwise."

"You know I can't," I replied. "I don't have money, and we're illegal here. Do you have any doctor colleagues, a psychiatrist, who could help us?"

"Actually," she started hesitantly, "I'm not a doctor."

"Oh, I'm sorry," I apologized. "Uncle Jamal told me you came to the UK to study medicine (MBBS)."

"He was right," she admitted. "But you might know that I got married and... well, I met him at a friend's party. We fell in love... or what I thought was love. I got distracted from my studies, and we married and had a child... so I never finished my education. I wish I could help you financially, but my financial situation is not good either."

"I understand," I said sympathetically. "Where is your husband, by the way? Is he at work?"

"I don't know where he is," she confessed. "We had an affair, and we got divorced. Baba was right. He wasn't a good person. After two terrible years, we separated. It was my mistake. I was naive. I felt ashamed that I fought with Baba for that person. I never got a chance to apologize to him." Tears welled up in her eyes. She wiped them away, and unsure of what to do to distract her, I asked about the photo of her daughter.

"She's... my precious daughter," Layla said softly. "She's never gotten to meet her father. I knew he was cheating, but I still wanted to be with him for her sake. But he abandoned us. One day, he just appeared with divorce papers, and here we are now. Last year, she was diagnosed with autism."

Tears streamed down her face now.

"Excuse me," she said, getting up and walking away. I stared at the photo of her and her daughter, a wave of pity washing over me.

CHAPTER 19

Tears welled in my eyes as I watched Zariya sleep. The room was shrouded in darkness except for the dim glow of the table lamp, which cast long, unsettling shadows on her face. It was a peaceful darkness. Even in sleep, the lines etched on her face, barely noticeable a year ago, seemed deeper now. Each wrinkle was a testament to the pain she bears. She was whispering something that I couldn't hear. I moved closer. She was chatting with Aleha's name.

Three months. Seven countries. The agent's words kept ringing in my ears, mocking our naive optimism. 'Travel light,' he had advised. But what could we have possibly left behind? Memories? Hope? Those were the only things we truly owned. We walked, my feet protesting against the harsh ground, our worn-out shoes offering little comfort. Days were spent navigating familiar roads, but nights were a terrifying plunge into the unknown wilderness. The wind howled relentlessly, rain whipped down like a thousand lashes, and the occasional monsoon left us shivering and drenched. Yet, fear consumed me more fiercely than any wild creature lurking in the darkness. We weren't alone in our suffering. There were many people who faced similar hardships. Some couldn't withstand the unrelenting hunger and thirst. Others, broken in spirit, gave in to despair, captured by the authorities we were escaping. What happened to them remains a chilling mystery, their stories lost in the whispers of the wind. And those who remained, fuelled by a flicker of hope, were plagued by constant regret. Every step forward felt like betraying everything we knew, a desperate gamble for a future that seemed to fade like a mirage with each sunrise. Every creak of the floorboards and every rustle of leaves outside the window sent shivers down our spine. Sleep offered no escape, only haunting echoes of the horrors we'd witnessed. We yearned for a humble meal, a cozy bed, and a moment of safety. Each day, we managed to have something to eat, even if it was just one or two dates after walking for miles.

But all this suffering pales in comparison to the loss of Aleha. It was entirely my fault. This decision to come here... now I have nothing to lose. My Zariya, I have to do something. I can't lose her. I've already lost everything. Right or wrong doesn't matter anymore. I'll do what I have to do at this point. I'm already late, but I can't afford to delay any further. Before I lose the last thing in my life...

I stood up with newfound resolve, a plan forming in my head. I knew what I had to do now. Opening the door, I left the room. Passing Layla, we exchanged glances, both of us holding a glass of milk for Zariya.

"Please think about what I said," Layla pleaded.

Her words only solidified my resolve to go back to the Warehouse.

CHAPTER 20

I walked closer to the main gate of the warehouse. I was not nervous or afraid, but there was a fire inside me, fuelling me to burn the whole world down without thinking of the consequences. Four to five guards were standing at the main gate... two of the guards had radios, and all of them had proper Bludgeons in their hands. One main guard is sitting in a small cabin with a radio and a gun. A few steps away from the gate, the guard stops me.

"I want to see the Boss."

"You are not allowed here."

"Go back!" the guard yelled. The Security Guard pushed me back again. I step forward again step forward without a flinch.

"Please let me go in... I need to meet him. It is very important. I kept my tone aggressive."

Another security joins us now.

"I told you, he won't meet you... just go away..."

The security guard shoved me with surprising force. I stumbled back, hitting the ground with a thud.

"You were wrong, Baba," I muttered, a surge of anger rising within me.

It fuelled my movements as I sprang to my feet, years of muscle memory kicking in. I'd been a martial arts teacher for seven years. It all started as fun when I was just nine years old. After twelve years of dedicated training, I told Baba about my dream of opening a martial arts academy. He wasn't supportive. He pointed to all his successful friends—doctors, Harvard graduates, lawyers, and engineers. "You'll bring shame to the family by fighting," he argued. "What will I tell my friends? That my son breaks people's necks? It won't benefit you. Your life will be wasted. Become a doctor or a lawyer. Help people. Be useful." But Baba was wrong. It wasn't useless. This wasn't about breaking necks; it was about protecting myself, protecting Zariya.

Two security guards, broad-shouldered and menacing, charged at me. I sidestepped the first guard's clumsy swing, launching a precise roundhouse kick with a satisfying thud on his chest. He stumbled back, gasping. The second guard lunged, but I ducked beneath his arm, using the momentum to spin and deliver a sharp elbow strike to his jaw. He crumpled to the floor, unconscious. The remaining guards hesitated, a flicker of fear in their eyes. I pressed my advantage, a whirlwind of controlled fury. I weaved through their attacks, deflecting blows with forearms hardened from years of blocking. A spinning backkick caught one guard on the knee, eliciting a yelp of pain. Another received a swift palm strike to his pressure point, sending him to his knees, doubling over. The chaos drew the attention of the head of security, a burly man with a shaved head and a cold glint in his eyes. He emerged from the building, a pistol glinting ominously in his hand. He barked an order for me to stop, but I ignored him, my focus solely on the remaining guards.

"Cut the act!" The head of security, a bulldog of a man, barked. "Put your hands up, and don't even think about moving."

A cold smile played on my lips. "Not going to work on me."

Slowly, I raised my hands, palms facing him. It was all a show. As I inhaled deeply, a plan ignited in my mind. With a lightning-fast movement, I dropped low, pivoting on one foot. In a fluid motion, I disarmed him, wrenching the gun from his surprised grasp. My other hand clamped around his neck, a firm but precise pressure point hold I'd honed over years of training.

"Open the gate," I rasped, my voice laced with steely resolve.

Trepidation gleamed in the security chief's gaze. He clumsily handled his keys, the metal jingling anxiously. A wave of relief washed over me when the gate clicked open. Still gripping him firmly, I forcefully pushed him towards the opening. A well-executed kick sent the gate swinging wide. A final, satisfying punch to the security chief's arm served as a reminder of the trouble he had caused. Without wasting another breath, I charged through the entrance, the warehouse looming large ahead. I hurried forward, navigating through the labyrinth of crates and pallets. I pressed on until, finally, a familiar figure emerged from the shadows. It was Steven.

"Hey! Hey, mate! Where are you going? How did you enter the premises?"

"I want to see the boss. It's urgent."

"I knew you'd come back here one day. But this early... I didn't think of that."

"Cut the crap and tell me where the boss is."

"Relax, mate!" He signaled you towards the boss's office. "His office is this way..." A long, congested alley. Only one person could cross at a time. I followed behind Steven. He stopped in front of a wooden door and knocked. "Wait here." He knocked again and went inside. I stood leaning against the wall. In a few seconds, he was out. "Come in."

I entered the room. It was small, with a glass table in the middle filled with files and two large computers. The boss sat in a comfortable maroon leather chair, wearing... (describe the rest of his clothing). A fire crackled in the fireplace, making the room warm and cozy. There were no other lights on in the room except the one above the table, which illuminated the space. Steven left, closing the door behind him. I sat in the chair across from the boss, facing him. He spat into a vase in front of him.

"Steven was sure you'd definitely come back," the boss said. "I'm happy you made the right decision."

"Boss, I need a job. I can do anything... anything. But I want to make a lot of money."

"Sometimes in life, you have to do things you never imagined for survival," the boss replied thoughtfully. "Hmmn," he grunted, expressing surprise. "I like that attitude."

He opened a box in front of him, took out a betel quid, and put it in his mouth. He cleaned his hands by rubbing them together. He relaxed back in his chair, then spoke after a moment's consideration.

"I have a job, but it's very difficult and dangerous. If you're caught, you'll spend the rest of your life in prison."

"What will the reward be if I succeed?" I asked without hesitation.

"A handsome amount of money," the boss promised.

"I'll do it," I said.

"Are you sure?" the boss asked. "I suggest you think twice. We won't take any responsibility if you're caught."

"I've made up my mind," I said. "I don't care about anything. All I know is that I want to give my wife a good life. That's it."

"Okay," the boss said. "If you've decided, then we'll proceed."

The boss made a call from the landline. In a few minutes, Steven came to the office.

"Yes, boss!" Steven said.

"You don't need to look for a delivery professional anymore. Rayan will deliver the stuff." He pointed his finger toward me and then spat in the vase again.

"But boss, he's inexperienced," Steven argued. "How can he deliver? He'll definitely get caught."

I looked at Steven and assured him, "Don't worry about that. I won't get caught. Trust me, I won't let you down."

Steven showed me where I had to deliver the parcel

"Listen, Rayan," the boss said sternly. "The path you're going on is a one-way street. There's no room for mistakes. Mind it."

"I know," I replied.

"You can go now."

CHAPTER 21

Steven and I were in an old model car. I had no idea where we were heading, but the evening scene was serene. Streetlights cast an orange glow on the broad road, flanked by large villas on both sides. Steven drove in silence. After a few moments, he pulled the car over to the side of the road.

"We're here," he announced.

"Where do I deliver the parcel?" I asked

"You have to drop it off at this gated community," he replied, gesturing towards a large complex.

A sign identified it as 'High Land Enclave.' It was a sprawling development, presumably home to the city's elite. High-security measures surrounded the entrance. Two or three police cars were parked outside the gate, and six or seven policemen stood guard, armed and holding radios. Two of them wielded metal detectors, while another held a sniffer dog trained to detect drugs and explosives. Inside the gate, another two or three armed police officers patrolled. A metal detector gate stood as an additional barrier. The policemen meticulously checked every car entering the complex. Most vehicles seemed to have passed, allowing them to proceed without further inspection. CCTV cameras monitored the entire area, and two police officers sat inside a small cabin, keeping a watchful eye on the feeds.

"This is High Land Enclave," Steven explained. "All the elite class—the super-rich, some ministers, and high-ranking government officials live here. It's a highly restricted area. You need to pass through the gate without getting caught. If they apprehend you, consider us strangers. You'll face life imprisonment. Do you think you can pull this off?"

I closed my eyes, and Zariya's face flashed before me. There was no turning back.

"Consider it done," I said confidently. "Don't worry about it."

"When do you need to deliver the parcel?"

"I'm ready now."

"Good. Me too." Steven started the car. He put his foot on the gas, accelerating the car back onto the main road and speeding away.

CHAPTER 22

We stood before the Boss in his office. He opened a black briefcase and slid it toward me on the table. "These are the drugs," he said sternly. "This bag is worth 1.5 million pounds. We're giving this to you with trust. Don't even think about cheating us. Otherwise, you'll be leaving the world very soon. Steven will be with you at all times," he added, spitting into a nearby vase.

"Don't worry," I assured him, determined. "Your parcel will be delivered safe and sound."

"Did you get the things I requested?" I asked.

"Yes, they're downstairs."

"Okay, Boss. I'll take my leave."

I zipped the bag shut, grabbed it, and started to leave as the Boss watched my back. "Good luck!" he called after me.

"Luck isn't enough for success," I countered. "A good strategy will work better."

He smiled in response.

We left the office, and I followed Steven downstairs. We entered a large but empty room in the warehouse. There was only a bicycle, a small toolbox on the floor by the side, and a small cotton bag. I placed the bag of drugs on one side, picked up the toolbox, and began to work on removing the bicycle's handlebar. After some effort, I successfully detached the handlebar. Then, I tore open the drug packets one by one and stuffed them into the empty handlebar tube. After finishing all the packets, I also stuffed some cotton into the hole. Finally, I reattached the handlebar and tightened it securely. To test my work, I then rode the bicycle around the room.

CHAPTER 23

I inched closer to the Minister's Enclave. The bag hung precariously on the bicycle handlebar. Steven remained in the car, keeping a nervous eye on me as I approached the gate.

A policeman approached me. "I'm here to deliver this bag," I announced, trying to sound confident.

"What's in the bag?" he inquired.

"Important documents," I lied smoothly.

"For which phase?"

"Phase Two," I replied, hoping I remembered the correct term.

"Get off the bike and park it to the side," he ordered.

I dismounted immediately, parking the bicycle a calculated distance away. Two more policemen materialized beside us, one holding a sniffer dog and the other wielding a metal detector.

"Search him thoroughly," one of them barked.

The first policeman took my bag and unzipped it. He scanned it with the metal detector, then meticulously searched its contents by hand. He ordered me to remove my coat and shoes, examining them as well. Finally, the sniffer dog came over, circling me and sniffing intently. Its bark erupted as it reached the bicycle. My breath hitched in my throat. The security personnel swarmed the bike again, searching every inch, but to no avail. Relief washed over me as they finally waved me through the gate. The policeman signaled for the gate to open, and I cycled through, my heart still pounding.

CHAPTER 24

"What happened? Did you deliver the parcel?" Steven bombarded me with questions as soon as I got into the car.

"Don't worry, the job's done," I replied calmly.

"Really? Oh yeah... haha! Excellent job, dude!" Steven exclaimed, a mixture of excitement, surprise, and happiness evident in his voice. He even pulled me into a hug. "But how did you do that? They checked you thoroughly, and even the dog sniffed you. How the hell did they miss the drugs?"

I smirked. "That's what we call magic. I'll teach you one day."

"I'm dying to know how you got through that gate undetected. Please tell me."

"Okay, okay. So, when you gave me the bag, I went down to the hall..." I explained every detail of how I'd hidden the drugs in the bicycle.

"Awesome, man! You're a genius! The boss is going to be ecstatic!" Steven cheered. "Sometimes, the simplest things give you the best results."

"Welcome to the team," he added.

"Thanks, Steven," I nodded, though a pang of guilt stabbed at me. I wasn't happy about this life, not at all. In fact, I felt ashamed. If Baba were alive and saw me doing this, he would have been heartbroken. Steven started the car, pulling onto the main road with a screech. He drove fast, his happiness spilling over into his driving. All the way back to the warehouse, he whooped and hollered with excitement. Once we arrived, I immediately headed for the boss's cabin. I knocked and entered. The boss looked up and smiled upon seeing me. He rose from his chair, spat in the vase as usual, and walked towards me with outstretched arms.

"Welcome, Rayan! Welcome!" he boomed, pulling me into a hug. "You did a great job, Rayan. I wasn't expecting that on such short notice. Congratulations! Sit, Rayan, sit. I have two surprises for you."

"What kind of surprises, Boss? Life is already throwing surprises at me every day," I replied with a hint of bitterness.

"No, no, these are the good kind," he assured me.

He opened the top drawer of his desk and pulled out a plastic bag. Inside were a cell phone and three bundles of cash. He placed them on the table in front of me.

"This is for you," he declared. "Your reward. Consider it just the beginning."

I reached out and touched the money, the feel of it triggering conflicting emotions. This kind of money could have saved Aleha if she were still alive. I picked up one bundle of notes and the cell phone.

"Take these two as well," the boss urged.

"One is enough for now," I insisted. "But, Boss, I need a place to stay."

"Yeah, sure. I'll arrange something for you."

"Thank you, Boss. I'll take my leave now."

"Wait, one more thing." He opened the lower drawer of his desk and retrieved a small pistol, placing it on the table next to the money.

"I don't need this, Boss," I said.

"Take it," he insisted. "You'll need it in the future."

With a heavy heart, I took the pistol. A nagging feeling told me he was probably right.

CHAPTER 25

I was driving the car with Zariya in the passenger seat. I told her we were moving to a new place, that I had money now, and that the boss had given me a car. But she didn't respond. Ever since Aleha's death, Zariya hadn't spoken a word. Her silence was killing me. I'd tried everything to get her to talk, but she just stared blankly at me. Finally, I pulled the car into the driveway of the house the boss had arranged for us. We reached our new home. It was a two-story house nestled in the middle of a jungle, surrounded by tall trees instead of other houses. I opened the car door for her and gently took her small, soft hand in mine. Leading her to the main door, I pulled out the keys and offered them to her. I wanted her to open the door of our new home. She hesitated at first but eventually unlocked it and walked inside.

The house was beautifully decorated and well-furnished. Upon entering, we found ourselves in a large living room with gleaming marble floors. A huge LCD TV covered most of the wall, facing a lavish brown leather sofa and a large, rectangular two-story glass table. A grand chandelier illuminated the entire room. Wide stairs ascended at the far end, which led to an open kitchen with a spacious marble countertop.

"Do you like the house?" I asked, but she wasn't even looking around. Her gaze remained fixed on the floor. "Aren't you curious about how I got this house? Where did the money come from? Or what kind of job I'm doing?"

She remained silent, staring at the floor, her silence growing heavier on me with each passing day. Back when we could still argue, she used to go silent to get me to apologize, knowing I hated it. Her silence always terrified me somehow. I'd rather have her yell or fight with me as long as she spoke.

Desperate, I knelt and held my ears, pleading with her, "Sorry, sorry." But she wouldn't even look at me, her gaze glued to the floor. Layla was right; I should take her to a hospital.

That's when my phone rang. It was Steven.

"Hello, Rayan, it's Steven. Where are you?"

"I just dropped Zariya off at home."

"Okay, then come to the shopping mall. We need to get you some things."

"Shopping for me? I don't need anything," I protested.

"You do! I'm waiting. Come quickly."

Kissing Zariya's forehead, I made her sit on the sofa, turned on the TV, and gave her a glass of something (you can specify what it is). Then, I headed out towards the mall, not forgetting to lock the door from the outside.

CHAPTER 26

Steven was waiting for me by the mall entrance, anxiously checking his wristwatch.

"Where have you been, man?" he asked when I finally arrived. "I've been waiting here for a long time!"

"Sorry, mate!" I replied.

"Let's go in," he suggested.

We entered the mall. I was astonished by its size. People bustled everywhere, shopping and chatting. Kids played in designated areas. Steven pointed towards a shop, and we headed there. Steven examined different dress shirts and coats, asking me to try them on. I was hesitant at first, but after his second request, I went to the fitting room. I came out a moment later.

"The dress shirt looks good on you," Steven said. We decided to buy it.

Next, we entered a perfume shop, where both of us tested different fragrances. We also browsed through a selection of glasses, trying them on in front of the mirror. Finally, we left that shop and moved on to the next one. Our exploration ended at a cafe, where we enjoyed snacks and coffee.

Leaving the mall, I accidentally collided with a passerby, a wayfarer. It was a forceful collision, and the wayfarer fell to the ground.

"Sorry!" I exclaimed.

The wayfarer's response was harsh. "Are you blind or what? Don't you know how to walk?"

"I already said sorry!" I replied.

The situation escalated. The wayfarer accused me of doing it deliberately and used offensive language. Infuriated, I grabbed his collar.

"Mind your language!" I demanded.

Steven intervened, trying to separate us, but I wouldn't let go.

The wayfarer dared me to hit him, calling me names. In a moment of uncontrolled rage, my hand moved instinctively, and I slapped him.

Enraged further, the wayfarer threatened me and my family. Overcome by a surge of violence, I pulled out my pistol and fired three shots at the wayfarer. The bullets hit him in the heart, ribs, and stomach. The wayfarer died instantly. Screams erupted as people witnessed the shooting and fled in terror. "You wanted to kill my family?" I yelled at the dead body, my voice laced with desperate denial. I was consumed by a horrifying realization of what I had done. Steven, gripped by fear, urged me to leave. We rushed towards our car. Steven, in a hurry, threw the shopping bags onto the back seat, jumped into the driver's seat, and sped away with a stunned me beside him.

CHAPTER 27

Two hours crawled by as Steven steered the car down deserted roads. The sun dipped below the horizon, casting long shadows across the desolate landscape. Finally, he pulled the car over onto a gravel shoulder, the engine sighing to a rest. He climbed out, his face etched with worry. "Stay inside!" he instructed, a low urgency in his voice. He dialed a number, his silhouette pacing restlessly next to the car as he spoke in hushed tones. After a brief conversation, he ended the call and slid back behind the wheel.

"The city's not safe for you anymore," Steven said, his voice grim. "The cops will be on the lookout. We're heading to a safe house." He didn't elaborate further; he just gripped the steering wheel and took off.

The road deteriorated as we ventured deeper into the countryside. Dust plumes billowed behind them as we navigated rough patches and tight curves. Finally, we emerged into a clearing, a small, unassuming house nestled amongst the trees. It seemed untouched by time, a solitary haven in the vast expanse of the forest. Steven parked in front, the engine ticking as it cooled.

They got out, the silence broken only by the chirping of crickets. He approached the house cautiously, the weathered wooden door creaking open with a groan. A wave of stale air and dust greeted them as they stepped inside. Dim light filtered through grime-coated windows, revealing an interior that hadn't been used in a long time. Cobwebs hung from the corners, and furniture was shrouded in dust sheets. A cough escaped us both as dust motes danced in the air.

"This safe house hasn't been used in a while," Steven explained, his voice echoing in the emptiness. "That's why it's so dusty."

His phone buzzed. He answered it, his voice guarded. "Yeah, we're here. Sending you the location now. Pick me up," he spoke into the receiver before hanging up.

"Who was that?" I asked, my voice barely a whisper.

"Just a friend," he replied vaguely.

Steven moved from room to room, a determined glint in his eyes. I followed, the floorboards groaning under my weight. Each room seemed untouched, a snapshot of a life paused in time. Finally, he led me into a bedroom.

"You don't need to worry about anything," he said, his voice reassuring. "No one knows about this place. You're safe here. Don't leave until I tell you it's okay."

A wave of gratitude washed over me. "Thanks, Steven," I mumbled, my voice thick with emotion.

"No worries, mate," I replied with a tight smile.

Suddenly, the sound of an approaching car broke the silence. Steven exchanged a glance with me, a flicker of relief in his eyes.

"That must be him," he said, gesturing towards the window.

Together, we moved towards the window, peering out into the gathering darkness. A car sat parked in the driveway, headlights casting a pool of light onto the dusty gravel. Steven hurried outside, the screen door slamming shut behind him. A moment later, I saw a figure emerge from the car, carrying two bulging shopping bags. It was a man, his face obscured by the shadows. Steven walked towards him, accepting the bags with a brief nod.

"This should be all the essentials you need," he said to the man, his voice barely audible through the window. Steven invited him. At the door, he handed me the paper bag. There was a burger inside. We sat around the table and started eating. As I took the first bite of the burger, a memory of Zariya struck me. How could I forget about her? She's alone! I locked the door, and she had nothing to eat. I could barely swallow my bite."I need to go. Give me the car keys!"

"Are you crazy? The police must be looking everywhere right now! Where the hell are you trying to go at this time? Sit down!"

"I can't sit down, Steven! Try to understand! My wife is alone at home! I locked the door from the outside! She has nothing to eat, and it's already night. She must be scared! Her mind isn't stable either, and I fear she might harm herself!"

"Okay, but let's go together. It's dangerous outside. You just killed a man, do you get it?"

"I know about that. Let me leave you alone. I'll be safely back in two or three hours. I'll take her to

Layla's house. She's my uncle's daughter, and she can definitely take care of her while I'm away. I promise I'll be back safely. Let me leave!"

He gave me instructions, then handed me the keys. "Drive safe."

I thanked him, took the keys, and made my way to the car. It was a black BMW 335. I got into the driver's seat and headed towards the house.

CHAPTER 28

Two policemen were patrolling the road when one of them spotted me driving the car. I tried to remain calm and composed, acting normal as I slowly passed them in my car. The policeman gave me a detailed look before continuing on. I parked the car in front of the house. I scanned the surroundings before getting out, then walked briskly towards the main door and hurriedly opened it. Zariya ran towards me, hugged me tightly, and started crying loudly.

"I've been waiting for you for a long time! You came very late. I hate you! You left me here alone. Where were you? I'll kill you! I was so scared and hungry too. I heard wolves howling, and I was afraid they'd attack the house. There's a jungle around here, and there must be dangerous animals. How could you leave me alone in this place?"

It was a sigh of relief for me. It was the first time in my life that I liked her scolding me, and I didn't want her to stop. Every word was music to my ears. I gently patted her head.

"Sorry! Forgive me. This will be the last time."

"Promise you won't leave?" She asked.

"Such a silly thing to make a promise for. I won't leave you ever." I pushed her away from my chest and held her in my arms.

"Are you hungry?"

She nodded no while wiping the tears from the back of her hand.

"Okay, No Problem. You'll be hungry in a few hours. I'll make you something to eat."

We sat down. I was genuinely happy that Zariya was talking after such a long time, and I hoped she might recover from the trauma soon. Suddenly, I heard police sirens getting closer to the house. Fear gripped me. I knew they were coming for me.

I stood up, placed the gun on the table, and prepared to leave.

"This is just for your safety... Use it if you need to... I have to leave now."

"This gun? I don't need it. Where are you going?"

Ignoring her questions, I immediately made my way to the door. I heard Zariya yelling and crying, begging me not to leave her alone. I hesitated several times, wanting to stay, but I knew if I didn't go, it wouldn't just be this one night. Zariya would have to spend all her nights alone in this house.

CHAPTER 29

I felt an overwhelming sense of guilt, like a hungry beast tearing at me from within. Leaving Zariya alone, especially after all she had been through, weighed heavily on my conscience. But the sound of sirens in the distance left me with no choice. I hurriedly left the house, the weight of the lifeless body serving as a chilling reminder of the night's events. My main focus was to conceal the person's identity. I frantically searched for something, anything, to cover their face. Suddenly, the piercing sound of a police car's siren filled the air. Adrenaline surged through me as I made a desperate move. I jerked the steering wheel, tires screeching in protest as I swiftly crossed the road, blending into the shadows. The police car raced by, its spotlight briefly illuminating the empty street. My heart pounded against my chest, each second feeling like an eternity. As the red glow of the police car faded into the distance, I cautiously looked back. Relief washed over me—they were gone.

But the relief I felt was short-lived. I ran as fast as I could towards my car, barely visible in the darkness.

I dove into the driver's seat, slamming the door shut and struggling with the ignition. The engine roared to life, echoing the turmoil I felt inside. I peeled out of the driveway, glancing nervously in the rearview mirror. My breath caught in my throat. In the distance, the red and blue glow of police sirens flickered like menacing eyes. They had spotted me. Panic surged through me. I pressed down hard on the accelerator, pushing the car to its limits. The engine protested with a high-pitched whine, but I didn't care. Every ounce of my being was focused on one thing: escape. The world around me blurred into a chaotic whirlwind of streetlights and rushing asphalt.

As I glanced at the side mirror, I could see the flashing lights of the police cars closing in on me. They were like sleek, menacing predators chasing their prey. The piercing sound of the sirens filled the night, haunting and relentless. At that moment, reason abandoned me. I felt like a cornered animal, driven by an instinctual need to survive. My eyes caught sight of a side road, and without thinking, I took a heart-stopping turn. The tires screeched in protest as I fought to maintain control. The car swayed and lurched, threatening to spin out of my grasp.

Suddenly, a massive truck loomed in front of me, illuminated by my headlights. It felt like time slowed down as I reacted in a split second. My foot slammed on the brakes, and a desperate prayer escaped my lips.

The world exploded in a chaotic symphony of screeching metal and shattering glass. The sheer force of the impact sent my car spinning in a sickening whirl. I felt weightless, suspended in a horrifying dance of destruction. And then, darkness.

A searing pain shot through my body, jolting me back to harsh reality. I groaned, attempting to move, but a wave of agony crashed over me. I was trapped beneath a twisted mass of metal, my body broken and battered.

Amidst the haze of pain, I could hear distant voices and see flashing lights. Police officers appeared around me, their expressions grim. Escape was no longer an option. The will to fight had drained away, replaced by a profound sense of defeat. This was the end.

As I drifted in and out of consciousness, a single thought emerged: Zariya. Memories flooded my mind—stolen glances in a crowded room, the nervous delight of seeing her for the first time, the incredible joy of holding Aleha in my arms for the first time. We had envisioned so much—witnessing our daughter walk down the aisle and cherishing our grandchildren in our embrace. A life filled with happiness was abruptly snatched away. A tear escaped from my closed eyelid, tracing a gentle path down my cheek. My only wish, a silent prayer whispered on ragged breaths, was for Zariya to discover the happiness I could no longer provide.

Printed in Dunstable, United Kingdom